I0527309

Philip Syng Physick Conner

Sir William Penn, Knight, Admiral and General at Sea

Great captain commander of the fleet

Philip Syng Physick Conner

Sir William Penn, Knight, Admiral and General at Sea
Great captain commander of the fleet

ISBN/EAN: 9783337197285

Printed in Europe, USA, Canada, Australia, Japan

Cover: Foto ©Raphael Reischuk / pixelio.de

More available books at **www.hansebooks.com**

Sir William Penn, Knight,

ADMIRAL AND GENERAL AT SEA,

GREAT CAPTAIN COMMANDER

OF THE

FLEET.

ALBANY, N. Y.:
J. MUNSELL, STATE STREET.
1876.

Introduction.

PRESUMING that most Pennsylvanians, in common with myself, feel that proper interest in the great founder of our state which makes valuable a knowledge of his father, the valiant admiral, I offer the following slight memoir.

If I may claim the credit of being the first to condense into one volume the substance of what is now ascertainable in regard to Sir William Penn, I would not undervalue the biographical notices in the various cyclopedias; they, however, are brief, and in different degrees imperfect. On the other hand Mr. Granville Penn's *Memorials* is a work of such extended and thorough research, that it ranks among standard books of reference, having original authority.

Mr. Hepworth Dixon has said that Sir William Penn was one of the suppressed characters of English history, and that the discovery of Pepys was also the discovery of the admiral. I presume that the vindicator of the Founder means, not that Pepys's scandals unveiled the true character of Sir William, but that the unwarrantable tittle-tattle of the reckless yet amusing diarist, caused the issue of the knight's original journal, correspondence and memoirs, from which were gained a correct account of his services, and a just estimate of his character and high abilities in naval matters, with their influence in the great achievements of the Dutch wars.

For two centuries much obloquy has rested upon Penn for the failure at Hispaniola, in regard to which even Mr. Dixon, in his life of Blake, charges Gen. Venables with cowardice. An admiral should not be blamed for the failure of a general, while Venables, if incompetent, cannot truly be called a coward, advancing as he did, at the very head of his troops. Whether Penn's efforts to restore the Royal Family are to be called treason, or a natural outburst of wrongfully suppressed loyalty, will depend upon the roundhead or cavalier opinions of the reader.

Prejudice has customarily applied the term " Irish rebels" to all Irishmen fighting against Englishmen, even when, as in the Parliamentary wars, they were struggling for the king, while the English were battling against him. This curious perversion of the term should be borne in mind.

Since I have not added references to my authorities in foot notes, I subjoin a list of books consulted by me, each of which contributed some mite, at least, of fact or confirmation to this biography in addition to that gained from Granville Penn's *Memorials*, a work which, besides affording the most varied and particular account of the admiral, gives, as Mr. Allen, the author of the *Battles of the British Navy*, declares, the best history of the first and second Dutch wars.

That the Penns of Penn Lodge in Wilts, were descended from the ancient stock of Penn of Penn, county Bucks, is claimed by both families. The statement first made public by me, that the quondam monk William was the connecting link, is based upon family manuscripts. (P. 96 Common Place Book of the Hon. John Penn Jr., library of the Historical Society of Pennsylvania; Philadelphia.) The point is an interesting one, and should receive the attention of genealogists, since its confirmation from some original source, contemporary with his time, would be valuable.

AUTHORITIES.

Manuscripts of the Penn Family in the library of the Historical Society of Pennsylvania, at Philadelphia.

Publications of the Rolls Office.

Granville Penn's Memorials of Admiral Sir William Penn.

Biographies of Gov. Penn by Dixon and others.

Gov. Penn's Works.

Histories of Cos. Bucks, Wilts, and Gloucester.

Burke's Genealogical and Heraldic Works.

French   "   "   "   "

Allen's Battles of the British Navy.

Dixon's Life of Admiral Blake.

Memoirs of the O'Briens.

Pepys's Diary.

Evelyn's "

THE PENNS OF PENN.

THE family of De la Penne, ancient and patrician in France, was established in England during the reign of William the Conqueror. Receiving an estate in Buckinghamshire, the race became so firmly implanted that their very name rooted itself to the soil, and although the male line failed in 1732, an heiress carried on the succession to the Penn-Curzon-Howes, whose chief, Earl Howe, now represents the elder line of Penn.

Thus for eight hundred years have the Penns been lords of the manor of Penn. They had come Frenchmen and conquerors to England, and they went back Englishmen and conquerors to France, in the train of Edward III, from whose sword Sir John Penn received the honor of knighthood.

Some two centuries after Sir John had thus been rewarded for his valor, his descendant and representative in chief, David Penn, Esq., resided at the old hall, holding there, as lord of the soil, his court manorial. This lord of the manor of Penn had taken to wife, Sibyl, a daughter of the family of Hampden, a name then ancient, and made illustrious in the succeeding century.

Such was the family of Penn, when the tyrant of the land, Henry VIII, demanded the presence of the lady of the manor at his court. The king had set his eyes on Sibyl; was it with hatred or with love? It mattered not, in the end each was alike fatal. Doubtless there were many misgivings in regard to the royal notice, and the breast of Sibyl may not have been untroubled by the memories of what had been; the fortune and the fate of women whom the king had loved. What imaginings were too wild of a monarch so full of fancies and caprice? But the command was imperative; so with a brave heart, and doubtless a frame radiant with all the health and vigor of a country life, Sibyl appeared in the august presence.

But there awaited her neither axe nor crown: three motherless children, each a future sovereign, craved her tenderest care. The king intrusted to her his children; Edward, afterwards the VIth of England, Mary the Bloody, and the great Elizabeth ; and so well did she discharge the duty imposed that his majesty, in gratitude, bestowed upon her new lands and manors.

The Penns of Penn Lodge.

WHILE the Penns of Penn manor were thus growing richer in houses and lands, they lacked not children. Among these was one William, who being a younger son, and seeing no danger of the race failing for want of descendants, renounced the world, and taking holy orders, entered the monastery of Glastonbury.

And now but for Henry VIII, there would have been no valiant admiral, Sir William, no founder William, nor any Commonwealth of Pennsylvania. The king broke up the monasteries, and turned the monks adrift. Among them was this brother William. Though tyrant and insatiate, Henry proved, at least to the Penns, no ingrate. In addition to the favors already bestowed, he now granted to this quondam monk a portion of the forest of Braydon in Wiltshire. True this was paying Peter by robbing Paul, for the land had been taken from the possession of the abbey of Glastonbury.

And thus into the wilderness went William, even as generations later went his great descendant, to found a family, and give unto the land a name. Having builded a house he called it Penn-Lodge, and, being freed from his vows of celibacy, took unto himself a wife. Here, and at Minety in neighboring Gloucestershire, his descendants remained for some generations, not great in wealth, but of sufficient estate to maintain a respectable station among the county gentry. At length, however, this fortune failed them, and on the death of the then William Penn in 1591, his descendants were forced to sell their patrimony and betake themselves to an active life of commerce.

Giles, a grandson of this "patriarch of failing fortune," took to the sea, and being instrumental in releasing some Christian captives, was proposed as vice-admiral of a fleet destined to chastise the Algerines. His commission however was never filled, but King Charles I granted him one probably much more lucrative, that of consul to the Mediterranean ports.

Of his two sons George and William, both had lives remarkable. The elder having grown rich as a merchant in Spain, was pounced upon by the Inquisition, as heretic and sinner, torn from wife and fortune, tortured and expelled. He wandered back to England, where he died. To the younger, victory granted her brightest palms; and though fortune laid a peerage at his feet, he turned from it mortified and cast down by the inflexible, yet conscientious, conduct of his son.

The Young Admiral.

WILLIAM, the son of Giles Penn, was born at Bristol in the year 1621. His father having destined him for the sea, gave him a most careful training in his own ship, and so, when the king called for officers for his navy, the youth though yet under age, was found fitted for the rank of lieutenant, from which he was promoted to captain on reaching his 21st year. In 1644 he was commissioned to command the Fellowship of 28 guns, with orders to join the fleet of Admiral Swanley in the Irish seas.

King Charles and his Parliament were now at open rupture; and since the latter had been so fortunate as to secure the fleet, this division of it under Swanley was sent to blockade the Irish ports, and crush that nation's efforts to raise a navy in opposition to the dominant power of England. Ireland, like the larger isle, was the field of contending armies, and Swanley's mission embraced the succoring of the beleaguered town of Youghall.

There can be no doubt of Penn's early promise and great proficiency ; both in conquest and defeat he was ever found equal to the occasion. His rapid advancement to positions of trust and honor, during his early days, when being comparatively unknown he was no object of envy and jealousy, forms a marked contrast to the suspicion, contumely, and suppression, with which he was treated when his capabilities and talents were discovered and envied.

A captain at 21, he was made vice-admiral, *ad interim*, at 24, and as such commanded, during the time which intervened between the death of his predecessor in that office, and the arrival of his successor commissioned by Parliament, Capt. Crowther, to whom he gracefully resigned this important station. Seven months after this, however, in March, 1646, he was again appointed to the command of a squadron, and in 1647 the Parliament confirmed his commission as Rear-Admiral of the Irish seas. He was then 26 years of age.

But let us return to the year 1646, and the beleaguered town of Youghall, whose communication with the sea, Penn, as vice-admiral, was endeavoring to keep open. Here it was that he received the notice and esteem of the powerful Lord Inchiquin, of the ancient and illustrious house of O'Brien, together with that of the family of the Earl of Cork, and others of rank and influence, drawing them to him in lasting bonds of friendship; and it was here that fortune gave him his first narrow escape from instant death. Having sent his barge in pursuit of one belonging to the enemy, Penn with the governor of Youghall, Sir Percy Smith, and other officers of distinction, crowded together on the parapet of a fort, the better to watch the chase. The enemy noticing the throng, trained a piece of artillery upon it, and in an instant the shot dashed among them, dealing death and destruction from which Penn and Sir Percy alone escaped. Nine of their comrades were struck down, including the Lieutenant Colonels Loftus and Badnedge. The vice-admiral offered up thanks to God for his merciful preservation.

Having lost one frigate by the explosion of her magazine, and the fire of the enemy driving his other ships from the harbor, Penn, for a time, was forced to see a close investment of Youghall. At length, however, he succeeded in running a bark through the fire of the batteries, and her supply of provision and ammunition, together with a salute fired by the fleet, as though Penn had news of some great victory, so encouraged the besieged, that they sallied and did considerable execution on the enemy, who soon after retired from before the town.

Shortly after this event, Penn—who was vice admiral merely *pro tem.*—was relieved of that office by the arrival of Captain Crowther, whom the Parliament, as previously stated, had regularly commissioned to be second in command of the Irish fleet. Seven months afterward, Penn again received the command of a squadron of the above mentioned fleet, and as the place of vice-admiral was now permanently filled, he hoisted the rear-admiral's ensign.

He had already pillaged and burnt several places in Kerry, and although, in after years, these rapacities were specially alleged against him, it was with great unfairness, when we remember the object of these acts, namely, Ireland and the Irish, an excuse in other cases deemed amply sufficient for the perpetration of the most horrible barbarities.[1]

---

[1] It is gratifying to find, in the honored name of Washington, a protest against these atrocities; about this time a Col. Washington actually quitted the English service on account of the cruelties he saw practiced upon the Irish.

The Key of the Shannon.

N the north bank of the Shannon, and about seven miles from the city of Limerick, stood the castle of Bunratty. Its position commanded the passage of the river, and, moreover, its ancient walls contained the great and powerful O'Brien, Earl of Thomond. So valuable was considered the prize of this stronghold and its lord, that the Irish had already determined to surprise the castle, kidnap the earl, and compel his adherence to the cause of his nation. But his lordship was as wily as the pope's nuncio, Rinuccini; and while he remained within his ancestral walls, he caused his countess to reside in London. Through her his lordship was well apprised of the course of events, and the comparative strength of parties.

The Catholic part of Ireland, however, was just about seizing the earl and his stronghold, when

3

the Parliamentarians sent a force to secure both. This expedition consisted of a squadron under Penn, and a land force commanded by Lt. Col. McAdam. The vessels numbered seven frigates and one hoy, while the troops amounted to some six or seven hundred men.

Sailing up the Shannon they anchored before Bunratty. A trumpet was sent to demand the castle of his lordship. who after a short parley complied, and permitted it to be garrisoned from the fleet. Thus this great noble and his fortress were secured. for a time, to the Parliament.

With one ship stranded and almost lost, through the incompetence of its pilot, and provision already scarce, Penn and McAdam commenced the strengthening of Bunratty, in anticipation of the approach of the Irish forces.

Hampered by these conditions, and harrassed by the repeated threat of a descent of fire ships from Limerick, the sailors were kept constantly on the alert, foraging. pillaging, and assisting to man the works on shore.

From Penn's journal it is evident there was an island near Bunratty which, as a strategic point, was important. On this he caused works to be erected, supervising their construction himself, and manning them with his seamen. It seems these defenses received the name of Fort Penn.

McAdam having determined on making a reconnoissance, requested Penn's presence; but before the troops were put in motion, the Irish swooped down on the town of Bunratty with 120 horse and 300 foot, firing it and killing some of the English. But the commander of their horse, McGragh, being wounded and captured, they were put to flight, and a large number slain; after which McAdam and Penn[1] marched with 600 foot, 50 horse, and 2 cannon, to Six-Mile Bridge, where the enemy was intrenched to the number of 1400 men.

After a sharp conflict the Irish were driven out of their works, the town and district for miles round, as usual, burnt and plundered, when the English returned to Bunratty, where Capt. McGragh and a lieutenant, dying of their wounds, were buried with the honors of war, and the victors heard an edifying sermon from Penn's chaplain. It is grati-

---

[1] From the text of *Penn's Journal* it is difficult to decide positively whether the rear-admiral accompanied all of these inland expeditions; however, since the accounts of these transactions occur in his *Journal*, and he speaks as a participant, I presume he did.

fying to note that the wounded and captured Irish were not forgotten by their lieut.-general, Pursell, money and linen being bestowed by him upon them.

Encouraged by this success, Penn and McAdam laid their heads together to concoct a scheme whereby the rear-admiral was to land, draw the enemy upon him, and feigning retreat, give a chance for the lieut.-colonel to cut off the Irish communications, which done, both were to fall upon the *Paddies* and exterminate them. But *Pat* is hard to exterminate; indeed very hard. It can be done just to the uttermost point, but somehow or other one never gets beyond that.[1]

The general rule held good in this instance, the English slaughtered some *rogues* and burnt several homes, but, *God*, says Penn, sent a great storm of rain and wind which frustrated the chief design. Indeed, "*God*" appears to have been very inconsiderate in regard to the English at this time, for while he neglected to afford them an opportunity of slaughtering the Irish, he obstinately persisted in setting the hearts of the English so much against

---

[1] I respectfully submit to the Irish race the motto, "I still live," as suggestive of the past, appropriate to the present, and of the future —*Aspirant!*

each other, that Penn records the murder of five of McAdam's soldiers by their comrades.

The enemy, though driven from before Bunratty, did not fail to retaliate; and while Penn was feasting and saluting the Earl of Thomond, approached within a mile, and pouncing upon the castle of Cappah, carried it by breach and assault, together with that of Rosmonnahane, whose garrison was reported hanged, a just reward, as Penn avers, for their cowardice.

Nor did the Irish cease their efforts upon Bunratty, but readvancing with an army of six or seven thousand men, under McCarthy Viscount Muskerry, sat down before it, sending in a demand for its immediate surrender. This being refused, they commenced a regular siege. Earnest work now began on both sides, and Penn again had the honor of drawing the enemy's fire upon his person, escaping with the same good luck as at Youghall. Both night and day were passed in hot skirmishes, and though the enemy were at times checked and repulsed, they gradually but surely advanced their siege.

Having greatly exhausted the country, and the activity of the Irish rendering difficult the keeping of what cattle they had, it was determined to dispatch two ships to England, with a request for what, as yet, had never been granted—an ample supply of troops, provision and ammunition. Necessary as this step had become. it was with great unwillingness that Penn gave it his consent; for he doubted whether the captains would ever return, after getting well out of such a disagreeable place as was Bunratty and its neighborhood.

Nearer and nearer came the enemy's approach, and harder, both at the castle and the island fort, worked McAdam and Penn to check it. During the day the sailors served on land, and at night their boats swept round the fleet to intercept those of the enemy, or cut off the descent of fire ships. Thus the contest was progressing, when, on the 1st of July, Penn was summoned to Bunratty to concert measures with its commander, in view of the general assault believed to be imminent.

Arrived at the castle, he found its commandant in consultation with his officers in regard to some army matters. and therefore, with proper delicacy of feeling. abstained from approaching them, lest by doing so he might be charged with interfering in affairs out of his sphere. Upon the breaking up of the council, however, he joined the officers at dinner, during which the enemy concentrated a very heavy fire upon a portion of the works called Jefford's House. Assiduous as brave, Col. McAdam left the dinner table to encourage his men, now under fire in the building; he had scarcely entered the place, when one fatal shot struck him dead. Great was the consternation and sorrow of the soldiers, while his officers, in spite of Penn's remonstrance, seized upon and divided among themselves some treasure which by accident had fallen into the colonel's hands during the siege. McAdam was succeeded in command of the land forces by Major Hooper.

On the 9th of July the Irish so out-manœuvered the English as to succeed in enfilading their defenses with artillery. On the two following days they carried some very important works by assault, and caused the ships which lay near to retreat in a damaged condition. Though thus cut off from the castle, the island fort was still approachable, and to it Penn hurried, taking command in person. He strove, by every effort now left possible, to stem the torrent of defeat, and endeavored by an example of personal courage and assiduity to keep up the spirit of his men. But to no purpose; it was known that the castle was isolated with but three days ammunition, that its garrison would not stand to their arms, and so an utter hopelessness spread throughout the entire force.

A council of war being called, it was decided, as necessary for the safety of the fleet, to abandon the occupation of the island; this was done, its works first being destroyed. As the troops in the castle, had they been able, would gladly have made a precipitate retreat, Penn was gratified by hearing that the Irish were willing to let them go — even with the honors of war; "drums beating, colours flying, and musquet bullit in their mouths." But the alert enemy discovering the demoralized condition of the garrison, forced upon it terms of such humiliation, that Penn was excessively exasperated and mortified.

And so ended the siege, but not the labors of the navy, which now had to receive and bear away its comrades in defeat, together with a host of women and children expelled from Bunratty by the entrance of the victorious Irish. Thus burdened, Penn's squadron at length rejoined the admiral at Youghall. So long as there was occasion for fortitude, Penn had manfully maintained a brave front, and it was not till all was over, and he had brought the shattered expedition to a harbor of safety, that anxiety and disappointment could affect him. Now, however, their accumulated effect made him, for a time, ill and unfit for service. He soon recovered, however, and ere long had the gratification of receiving the captaincy of a perfectly new ship, and of hearing Parliament resolve that he had " Served with courage and fidelity," thus removing any shade of fault from his late arduous yet unsuccessful efforts.

William the Avenger.

FOR three long and weary years Penn's elder brother, George, had been held in durance by the Spanish Inquisition. Deeply as William felt his wrongs, he was helpless to relieve them, but an accident at length placed the power of retaliation in his hands. Among the many rich prizes of which his ship made capture, was the St. Patrick. On her he found a Spanish gentleman, Don Juan de Urbina. The opportunity of revenge for the torture which his brother had undergone, and might that very moment be suffering, was too good to be lost, and so Penn, stripping the Don stark naked, turned him over to the coarse buffoonery of the forecastle. This act appears to have had its desired effect — the awakening of the Spanish government to justice in behalf of George Penn, for soon after he was released from prison.

Beside the formal acknowledgment of his courage and services, Penn now (May 1647) received the

Parliament's confirmation of his rank as Rear-Admiral of Ireland. But not long after these honors had been conferred, he is found deprived of his ship and placed under arrest. The cause of this sudden fall cannot be given with perfect certainty, but it was most probably a suspicion of lingering loyalty to the Stuarts.

That Penn was ever faithful to his country, and never willingly disloyal to his king, appears evident.

In this instance, however, matters were soon rearranged, and Penn restored to his former command, from which he was eventually advanced to that of Vice-Admiral of Ireland. This last appointment was confirmed by Parliament on the 3d of March 1649, before he had completed his 28th year.

Heretofore although the Parliament had waged war in defense of its rights, it had not attacked the person of the king. Now, however, the violent faction getting the upper hand, his majesty, with all of royalty, was marked for destruction, while from the Commonwealth, Cromwell, as represented on the prow of the *Nasby*, in reality planted his heel on the neck of three Kingdoms. Feared abroad, he was dreaded at home, and the greatness of England in his day is comparatively mythical; Cromwell alone was great. The nation cowered in terror before the giant it had called forth. It is absurd, yet pitiable, that Republicans should sing pæans to the Lord-Protector.

The faction which arrested the king, and ultimately brought him to the block, found no friends in the navy. While the officers of that service never refused to fight for their country, even when usurpers ruled, they ever looked to an accommodation with the king. Aware of this sentiment, this patriotism which still cherished a spark of loyalty, the dominant party laid its hand upon the navy, to form it to its liking. Officers bred to the sea, were displaced, and in their stead were thrust landsmen. Such a course naturally excited dissatisfaction and resentment, and a large part of the fleet, expelling the land general imposed upon it, declared openly for the king. Fortunately no action took place between the sections of the divided fleet, and as the exiled Prince of Wales could not maintain a naval force, its officers, with his permission, subsequently returned to England, where their nautical skill prompted Cromwell to make use of them as drudges, to *coach* the unhorsed troopers whom he sent to sea as admirals. And thus while the navy did the work, the glory which should have been its own reward, was appropriated by the usurping military despots.

Fortunately for Penn, it is probable his timely arrest, in 1648, saved him from that personal humiliation which followed the overt acts of many of the most eminent captains and admirals. But nevertheless, he had to bear, in common with them, the general distrust and disfavor which rested upon the whole body of the regularly bred naval officers, and which, as above indicated, caused their supersedure, in all places of the highest command in the fleet, by the officers of the army. Galling as this was, their humiliating failure to avert, made it inevitable, and they were forced to endure. And so, like Sindbad, the navy carried the army on its back, to victory and fresh laurels.

And here I can not avoid calling attention to a strange incongruity, which displays itself in the English character, in regard to the naval victories of the Commonwealth; for while the Protestant English have ever been most infidel in regard to the insignificant *miracles* attributed to papal saints, they have, for more than two centuries, with unquestioning credulity, calmly swallowed the marvelous acts attributed to these landsmen afloat. Great victories, won over the most skillful and renowned admirals, are quietly set down to the blind bravery of, doubtless, half sea-sick landsmen. Verily one might cry; " *Credo*, the age of miracle had not then passed ! " were it not that through the glamour which well earned land victories raised around the soldier, is detected the arduous effort and steady courage of the seaman.

In all of these great naval victories, beneath the super-imposed bravery of the general, is found the seamanship and courage of some skilled sailor, and when the arrogance of the soldier set these aside, there followed defeat.

Sindbad the Sailor.

SUCH is the character which Mr. Granville Penn presents as representative of the navy under the rule of Cromwell, saddled as it was by the army. Land officers had usurped the place of admirals, and, as generals-at-sea, outranked in a moment old and trained naval commanders, whose positions had been reached by years of constant yet unostentatious toil.

Such even was Blake, who in common with the other soldiers brought, at least, no experienced seamanship to the navy; for the most careful biographer, and searching investigator of his life, gives not the slightest hint that he ever trod the deck of a ship at sea before his fiftieth year, when he suddenly received a chief command in the fleet. But Blake, unlike the others, was a genius. He was no more a trained soldier, than he was a trained sailor, yet, on land as on sea, he was ever victorious. True it is that his days of youth and first manhood were passed in close study; and who can say whether he did not then master the theory of that science which in after years embodied itself in actual victory?

With the most penetrative instinct he perceived how to add to his own being the element of nautical power by drawing around him, and knitting to his very soul, the ablest seamen of the fleet. Absorbing their natures, he became a true child of the sea. Thus as nature gathers the scattered drops of moisture, his soul collected to itself all the separated parts of naval force, and as the storm hurls back a deluge, he launched them forth in concentrated power.

After several years Penn was at length released from the Irish fleet, whose service of blockade and pillage his great grand-son justly calls tedious and hateful. In November, 1650, he received the command of a squadron whose active and important service was to chase and capture that of Prince Rupert. It was certainly a marked honor to be appointed to destroy this desperate rover.

But though Penn swept the channel, and penetrated the Mediterranean to a point hitherto ungained by an English fleet, the prince was so fortunate as to elude his pursuit. In this cruise the English ships proved themselves the fastest of sailers, and their commander never hesitated to make all foreign admirals, in the channel, strike to his their flags, exercising also the right of search.

These honors to their flag the English claimed by prescriptive right. dating from the days of their Saxon kings, when they were granted in grateful acknowledgment of the protection afforded by the English ships to the traders of all nations. In later times this once voluntary act of courtesy being demanded as a rightful acknowledgment of submission and vassalage due to the British, led to many contests, and among them our first war, as a nation, with England.

The Battle for the Flag.

AS the open seas which surround England dash their waters with concentrated and tumultuous force through the narrow channel which separates her from the continent, so the fleets of Europe surged together within its confined bounds. Here for ages had they met in constant rivalry and frequent battle, but the fierceness and magnitude of past contests was to be far exceeded by the great wars now opening.

Holland, as most powerful at sea, determined to annul the growing rivalry of England, and to abolish for ever "The Honour of the Flag." An occasion soon offered itself, and the Dutch refusing the customary salute to the English, were set upon by the latter and so severely handled that they were forced to yield. In the correspondence which followed between the two nations, neither would give way, and thus was ushered in the great naval war of the years 1652 and 1653.

The Dutch fleet, numerous and powerful, was commanded by admirals whose names alone seemed invincible: Tromp, De Ruyter, De Witte and Everetzen, while that of England was intrusted to Blake, Deane and Monk, generals-at-sea, Penn, Vice-Admiral of England, and Lawson, Rear Admiral. The Hollanders were not slow after open war had been declared, and catching Blake somewhat at disadvantage, pounded him so well that in mortification of spirit he tendered his resignation to Parliament, while Tromp, in exultant derision, placed a broom at his top-mast, and unchecked, swept the seas.

Humiliating as was this event it was not useless, for while Cromwell's good sense prevented him from permitting Blake to resign, it caused him to weed out the unworthy officers and to replace them by efficient ones; among the latter was John Lawson, whose valor and seamanship rightfully supplanted the mere military bravery of a soldier, as Rear-Admiral of England. In this substitution of a sailor for a soldier the counsel of Penn is presumed to have had great effect.

Thus reorganized the English navy entered upon that "year of wonders," 1653. During its course were fought some of the greatest of naval battles, the conflicts covering days, embracing hundreds of ships, thousands of men, and strewing the length and breadth of the channel with the wreck and ruin of fleets.

On the 18th, 19th and 20th of February, 1653, was fought the battle of Portland. The English attack was led by Penn in the *Speaker;* who, when the Dutch concentrated to crush the general's squadron, gallantly came to the rescue, charging with his whole division through the hostile fleet. He was greatly damaged by this intrepid act, but Lawson, Vice-Admiral of the Red, performing a similar one, and Monk's division now drawing near, Tromp, whose chief aim was the preservation of his convoy of over two hundred merchantmen, changed from an aggressive to a repellent attitude, and, with his men-of-war formed in a half moon around the merchant ships, proceeded up the channel. In this order, though hotly pressed by the English, Tromp at length brought his charge to a port of safety. Both sides had over 70 men-of-war engaged; the English lost 8 or 9, the Dutch 11, and 60 merchant ships; while the number of the dead and wounded of each fleet was great.

The nations now set to work to repair and increase their fleets, and by May the English had

105 ships, mounting 3840 guns and manned by 16269 sailors and soldiers.

On the 2d of June, 1653, Tromp, De Ruyter, De Witte, and Everetzen, appeared off the English coast with a fleet of 105 sail. The English at once bore down upon them with one hundred. A fierce battle ensued, in the height of which a cannon ball cut in two the valiant Gen. Deane. Monk took the cloak from his own shoulders, and threw it over the mangled body. At six o'clock in the evening the Dutch drew off, night intervened, and the morning of the 3d found the battle drifting towards the North sea. With the light the contest re-commenced, and now took place that brilliant passage-at-arms, the duel between the valiant admirals Tromp and Penn.

The Lieutenant-Admiral of Holland, singling out the Vice-Admiral of England, grappled with him, and poured his boarders into his ship. These Penn, by his valor, repulsed, and in his turn entered Tromp. So fierce was his retaliation that the Dutch were forced below; a moment of hesitation and Tromp and his ship were lost; with instant decision and reckless bravery he exploded some barrels of powder, hurling into the air his upper decks with all the invading English!

Terrible as this sight must have been to the crew of Penn's ship, it did not daunt their courage, but in fresh force, they actually reëntered the Dutch admiral. And now, indeed. his fate seemed sealed, but the admirals De Witte and De Ruyter, seeing the peril of their chief, came to the rescue, and Tromp was saved. Night again coming on, the defeated Dutch took refuge in the Texel. Their loss was great; 20 ships, 1300 prisoners among whom were six captains and two rear-admirals, while the English preserved every vessel of their fleet, suffering only in the loss of Gen. Deane, and 352 others slain and wounded.

So marked had been the ability displayed by Penn, that Monk personally pressed his advancement to the high position made vacant by the death of Deane, and thus he finally won the rank and title of General-at-Sea, an honor conferred on him alone of all the naval officers.

Great as had been this success, victory followed it with that decisive triumph, the first battle of the Texel. On the 29th of July the two fleets came in sight; that, and the following day, were passed in skirmishing, but on the 31st, Tromp, having the wind, bore down on the English. Each fleet numbered much over a hundred sail, and the line of battle extended some twelve miles. Grand indeed must have been the sight and terrible the combat, for it is recorded that the Dutch fought this fight with an increased fury, while the desperate charge of the English ships, led by Monk and Dakins, through their fleet, attests with what dashing bravery they were met. As the long line closed in a dense cloud of smoke shrouded the combat; broadside upon broadside flashed and roared from eight thousand cannons, while ever and anon flared the fire ships, followed by the terrific explosion of some great man-of-war. The sea was strown with dead bodies, broken spars and masts, while from out the gloom drifted shattered and dismantled hulls.

Tromp, ever eager for close quarters, bore down on Monk, hoping by his destruction to break the spirit of the English; but it proved his last onset; not victory, but death received him. With their great admiral passed hope from the Dutch, and they fled before the English.

The British lost 3 ships, and over 1300 men killed and wounded. The Dutch, besides Tromp, had 6200 men killed, wounded and captured, with 26 ships destroyed, and Admiral Everetzen a prisoner to the enemy. The conduct of both Penn and Lawson was distinguished as "very noble and renowned," and chains of gold were awarded them.

Tromp killed, Everetzen captured, peace, and the "Honour of the Flag," were the great trophies of this victory.

The Capture of Jamaica.

THOUGH war had not been declared against Spain, Cromwell determined to attack her, and therefore in the autumn of 1654 he sent a fleet under Penn, with an army under Venables, to prey upon the West Indian isles. The fleet consisted of 40 sail, while the army had a nominal force of 3000 foot and 60 horse.

Both admiral and general were, in common with many of their countrymen, now heartily sick of Cromwell's usurpation, so much so that their latent loyalty burst its wonted bounds, and each made separate offers of service to the Prince of Wales. The times, however, not being fully propitious they could not be accepted, and so the expedition sailed for the American seas.

These propositions were known to Cromwell, though at that time he took no notice of them;

6

but upon the unexpected return of the commanders in the following year (1655), he had both admiral and general committed to the Tower, for the alleged reason of disobedience to his orders; but as the official documents given by Mr. Granville Penn do not confirm this plea, it is highly probable the true cause was apprehension for his own safety in the event of Penn openly declaring for the Prince of Wales.

With this slight interruption I will now return to the year 1654, and the regular course of its events.

The expedition, though apparently formidable, was in reality wretchedly equipped and miserably organized. Indeed so poor were the *personel* and *materiel* of the army, that if we are to credit the great design attributed to it by Cromwell, the finger of derision and scorn may well be pointed at the infatuation, or culpable ignorance of its originator, the Lord-Protector. The fleet appears to have been in good order, but as its ships could not walk over the lands marked out for conquest, we note with contempt the helpless and pitiable condition of that force which could, the army.

In the first place instead of 3000 men, but 2500 left England; of these but 1600 were armed, and that with wretched muskets. Of 1500 guns promised but 190 came to hand, while the powder was of such a quality that it soon became useless. The increasing of the forces, by volunteers from the West Indian isles, to some 8000 men, added to the existing embarrassment; for owing to the want of muskets the recruits had to be armed with half-pikes, the making of which caused loss of valuable time, while the excess of mouths soon caused a scarcity of provisions, which, to the dismay of all, was found to be irreparable, even by the united efforts of Barbadoes and New England, while the *elan* of the troops was destroyed by the apathy of Gen. Venables, whom sickness deprived of that spirit and vigor necessary for a successful *coup*. Under these circumstances it is not surprising that they met with failure.

Having sighted San Domingo on the 13th of April (1655), the greater part of the army was landed without molestation at two o'clock Though the combined naval and military force of the English amounted to some eight thousand men, all of it, of course, could not be landed at once; probably about five or six thousand were thrown ashore, while the Spaniards brought a force perhaps equal, but not greater, in opposition. Pushing on, without either artillery, picks, or spades, but well provisioned from Penn's ships, the English approached Fort St. Jeronimo. General Venables, with a musket on his shoulder, marched with reckless bravery in advance of the column, when it was suddenly set upon from ambush. In their eagerness the enemy mistook the general and his two companions for mere privates, passed them by, and fell upon the advanced guard.

This saved Venables, who with one of his party joined the main body, his other companion being slain by a great shot from the fort. A severe skirmish ensued in which the Spaniards were repulsed. The army, however, could not hold its position, and in retreating it is estimated two or three hundred men perished from thirst, before reaching the river Hina.

Five or six days of comparative inaction now passed, when the army, this time provided with scaling ladders and a piece of artillery, again drew near fort St. Jeronimo. It was, apparently, the general's intention to carry the place by storm. The *forlorn hope* consisting of some hundreds of men, commanded by Capt. Butler and the adjutant-general, passed under the fire of the fort, and reaching a position free from its effect, were confronted by a sally, whose number was differently estimated at from 40 to 150 men.

The van of the *forlorn*, delivering its volley, wheeled handsomely, thus affording an opportunity for the rear to fire, which was done, but with no effect, for the Spaniards, with unchecked valor, charged upon it with their lances, driving the men pell-mell upon the *reformadoes*, who in turn were pressed in confusion upon the horse, and the whole mob, breaking through the general's regiment, bore its confusion into the ranks of the major-general's, where, however, it was checked by the steadiness of the sailors under Vice-Admiral Goodson. It is asserted that these hundreds of frightened Englishmen were put to flight by but forty brave Spaniards, while the staunchness of seven or eight sailors quelled the panic and repelled the pursuers. If true it affords a notable example of the wretchedness of cowardice, and the worth of courage.

One act of valor on the part of the English, however, deserves special notice : their major-general, Haynes, while endeavoring to rally his troops, was thus accosted by a huge mounted Spaniard : " What make you here, you English dogs ? I'll teach you to lead men !"

"Welcome, brave fellow!" cried the major-general, and encountered him with only his small sword, which, however, was so well played that the Spaniard drew off, but quickly returning with some lancers, slew that gallant officer, and two others who alone stood by him. One of these, Ensign Boys, feeling that he had received his death wound, stripped the colors from their staff, and wrapping them around his body, fell dead.

The panic being at length stopped, the troops bivouacked, and though no enemy disturbed them, such was their state of terror that the mere noise of the "crabs in the wood" drew forth wild volleys. In the morning it was found that besides many valuable officers killed, their force was reduced by one-eighth. A council of war being called, several officers were cashiered, among them the adjutant-general, who, besides, had his sword broken over his head for cowardice.

Into the hands of the Spaniards fell many muskets, five flags, and the *ashes* of the mortar carriage, which the English were forced to burn.

Penn was greatly provoked at the failure of the land forces, and offered to attack Fort St. Jeronimo and its batteries with his ships. Capt. Fernes also advocated the attempt, but on consultation with the army officers it was abandoned, since the demoralized condition of the troops would render abortive any attempt at capture, even were the forts silenced by the fire of the fleet. This belief, together with the apprehension of starvation, sickness, and damage to the ships from the approaching season of rain and storm, made their longer stay not only useless but actually dangerous, and so it was reluctantly decided to withdraw, and seek some other field of action, where, if successful, they could replenish their depleted stores.

Jamaica was fixed upon for their second attempt. On the voyage hither died Mr. Commissioner Winslow, heart broken at this first humiliating failure.

On Wednesday the 9th of May (1655), the island was sighted, and on the following day Penn, together with Venables, in the *Martin* galley of 12 guns, led the attack in person. Running bravely into the fire of the fort, the boats were cast off, and the army thrown ashore, where, to their astonishment, they found a fleeing foe. Thus, after trials and disappointments, a great prize dropped of itself into their hands.

A council being called it was discovered that as sufficient provision could not be procured for so large a force, all would ultimately have to abandon the island, unless the number of mouths was at once reduced. To effect this it was determined to despatch home immediately the greater part of the fleet, while three ships were ordered to New England for supplies. A committee being appointed to decide what vessels should go, and what stay, placed on the list for England that of the admiral, and so Penn, after putting Goodson in chief command of the ships to remain, sailed for home.

From the above fact it will be seen that those writers who accuse Penn of having deserted his post, speak ignorantly, for though he was commander-in-chief, and was endowed with discretionary power to decide his own movements when in foreign seas, he for the time waved that prerogative, and placed himself at the disposal of the committee.[1]

Another error exposed by the keen investigation of his great grand-son, is the assertion that Penn permitted the Spanish plate fleet to pass

---

[1] In objection to this it may be urged that a commander " must not leave his station ;" true, but suppose he is driven from it ? In this case he would most properly seek his nation's ports. Such was Penn's fate ; a necessity as inevitable as that arising from disastrous battle drove him back to England.

him unassailed; the truth is it never came near him.

Having reached London, Penn was committed to the Tower, under the charge before stated, but in reality to prevent all danger of his taking any action against the usurpation of Cromwell. Whatever step Penn may have contemplated was frustrated by his imprisonment, and when it was intimated to him that freedom could alone be obtained by the surrender of his commission as general-at-sea, and the making of his submission to Cromwell, he acquiesced. His descendant however asserts that in this transaction he did not humiliate himself as the official account represents.

Released from the Tower and dismissed from the service of the Lord-Protector, Penn, in the autumn of 1655, repaired to his estate in Ireland, where in common with other royalists he, at least, nourished the cause of the Stuarts.

With Penn both Ayscue and Lawson were set aside by Cromwell as of dangerous principles, and it is worthy of note that the latter in particular became the returning wave which gave the first shock to the Cromwellian domination, and carried in the renewal of legitimate monarchy. That the foundation of the restoration, though secured by

Monk and the army, was laid by Lawson and the navy, is shown by the researches of Granville Penn in his *Memorials* of the admiral.

Upon the death of their great master, the English people stretched forth their now free arms in yearning to their king, nor was their freed loyalty slow in rewarding those who had suffered in the cause. Penn was called from his retirement to represent in Parliament the town of Weymouth, and having hurried to Holland to bear in person the glad tidings of restoration, his majesty thereupon knighted him, making him also, in the following July (1660), a commissioner of the admiralty, and soon after governor of Kingsale, which office bore with it the title of Admiral of Ireland, while the estate of Shangarry was given to him in exchange for that of Macroom, restored to Mc Carthy earl of Clancarty.

The king having appointed his brother, James Duke of York, Lord-High-Admiral, that prince had the good sense to appreciate the worth of such an accomplished sailor as Penn, together with the fortitude to withstand, for a time at least, the efforts of the envious to supplant the admiral in the royal favor. In trained seamanship Sir William was of course the superior of Blake, whom in fertility of

resource and inherent talent for naval command
the knight, at least, so closely resembled, that Mr.
Dixon declares, upon the death of Blake, Penn stood
without a rival among the admirals of England.

From the incipient preparation, to the actual
sailing and fighting directions, the influence of this
thorough sailor can be plainly traced, while to learn
that he was with the duke at the great victory
over Opdam, is to know whose head planned, and
whose hand actually achieved that triumph.

THE GREAT-CAPTAIN-COMMANDER.

controversy having arisen between the Dutch and English in India, the two nations again declared war in 1665. The English fleet consisted of over a hundred sail, formed in three divisions, as indicated by the colors of their flags.

The white squadron was commanded by Prince Rupert, with Christopher Myngs vice-admiral, Robert Sansum rear; the blue, the Earl of Sandwich, admiral, Sir George Ayscue, vice, and T. Tiddiman, rear, while the red bore His Royal Highness the Duke of York, Lord-High-Admiral of England and commander-in-chief of the whole fleet. His vice-admiral was Sir John Lawson, his rear, Sir William Berkley, while in his royal highness's ship, the Royal Charles of 78 guns, was Sir William Penn, bearing the special title of Great-

Captain-Commander. The combined force numbered 22206 men, and 4537 guns.

The Dutch fleet consisted of eight squadrons, seven of which were brought into action. In numbers their ships fully equalled, and probably exceeded those of the English; while they bore over 4000 guns, and 20000 men. This armada was commanded in chief by Heer Van Wassenaer, Baron Opdam, Great-Admiral of Holland and West Friesland; its numerous squadrons were under the admirals Evertzen, Cortenaer, Stellingwerf, Cornelius Tromp, Cornelius Evertzen and Schram.

At dawn on the 3d of June, 1665, these two great fleets approached each other. Both were formed in parallel lines of battle, stretching some fifteen miles in length. On the English side Prince Rupert led the van, the Earl of Sandwich bringing up the rear, while the centre division, or *battle* was held by H. R. H., the Duke of York. The Dutch were led by the son of the great Tromp; followed by the admiral-in-chief.

Thus formed, the fleets passed, and repassed, delivering broad-sides at long range until 11 o'clock, when, the English having the wind, the Duke of York signalled to bear down on the enemy, which being done added fresh vigor to the conflict, and the red squadron, with Lawson now in the van, breaking through the Dutch line of battle divided their fleet, whose rear, cut off and out matched by the entire force of the British, was abandoned by its van, which incontinently fled.

The duke, with Penn at his side and surrounded by a brilliant group of noble volunteers, was singled out by a Scot, Sebastian Seaton, for his prize. The Scot, with the greatest valor, ran his ship aboard the prince, and would have entered him but for Sir Jeremy Smith and Rear-Admiral Tiddiman, who pouring in their fire killed Seaton's boarders, and forced his ship, the Orange of 75 guns, to strike. Many of the ships were now engaged yard-arm to yard-arm, and ever and anon the dense smoke of the conflict was rent asunder by the flaming course of the fire ships. The duke noticing the ship of the Great-Admiral of Holland, declared that "he would himself have a bout with Opdam," and bearing up engaged him.

Broadsides were exchanged, and at the delivery of the third from the duke, the Concord was hurled from sea to air by the explosion of her magazine, Opdam and all his crew perishing. This tragic act ended the battle : those ships of the Dutch not sunk or captured, fled before the English, who pursued them to the Texel.

The glory to the victors was overcast by a most sad casualty, the slaying by a single shot, and close to the duke, of the following young noblemen of valor and promise: the Earl of Falmouth, Lord Muskury, and a son of the Earl of Burlington. Other noblemen and brave sailors also met death, among the latter that courageous and able seaman Vice-Admiral Sir John Lawson.

One ship, with five or six hundred men killed and wounded, completed the English loss, while that of the Dutch numbered six or eight thousand killed, wounded and captured, while twenty-four ships were taken, burnt, or sunk. Among the dead, besides the Great-Admiral, were two lieutenant-admirals, and one vice-admiral. Thus ended this great battle. The Dutch fleet was commanded by the ablest of seamen, the renowned admirals of Holland. Its list of commanders is a roll of heroes; and yet, it sank in defeat beneath a fleet whose chief officers had never before seen a line of battle formed. Such were the Duke of York, Prince Rupert and the Earl of Sandwich, the two latter had seen sea service, and naval duels, but never before the manoeuvres and engagement of entire fleets.

So far as mere fighting was required, these soldiers were all-sufficient, but the vessels had to be handled so as to work in accord with the signals of the flag-ship, and engage properly and with advantage, and this was gained by such thorough seamen as Lawson, Ayscue, Jordan, Myngs and others, acting as lieutenants to the generals. Thus also was the proper manœuvring of the different squadrons assured, while the fighting, and united action of the whole, as one fleet, was secured through Penn, who though nominally under the orders of the Duke of York, was virtually commander-in-chief.

To Penn was referred the selection of the naval officers of that fleet, from him emanated its order of battle, and his was the hand which guided the Duke of York to victory. Its glory has long made that prince illustrious in the annals of naval warfare; while the honor, justly Penn's, should place his name on the roll of England's great admirals.

On the 8th of July following, Penn as Vice-Admiral of England, made his last cruise, in the fleet of the Earl of Sandwich, Captain-General of the Narrow seas. Upon his return to port he found that the navy was again doomed to act as Sindbad to the army, and so, being naturally jealous and careful of his well earned reputation, he requested and received a relief from service under the generals-at-sea.

Events soon turned out as he must have anticipated. Monk, though an able soldier, was a man obstinate, and greatly prejudiced against all naval tactics, holding them in contempt, and deeming untrained bravery alone sufficient for victories at sea. He met the Dutch, and was defeated with great loss of men and ships. To repair this disaster, and keep the elated enemy from burning London, now taxed Penn's efforts, and not only in this year, but particularly in the one following (1667). Though not by the Dutch, London was fated to be burnt, and when the great fire did sweep its sheet of flame over the metropolis, it found in Pepys a vivid chronicler, bringing us face to face with the terrified citizens, their houses burning and their goods piled in the open streets, while Sir William Batten, Sir William Penn and Master Pepys, hurriedly bury their wine, papers and other valuables.

During this year (1666) Penn's portrait was painted for the Duke of York, by Lely; it is now in the Greenwich gallery. He also received a pressing letter from his relative John Georges of

8

Bawnton Esq., M. P. for Cirencester, and Deputy Lieutenant of Gloucestershire, urging him to re-purchase his ancestral home of Penn-Lodge. This he for a time contemplated, but did not carry out, his Irish estates occupying his whole care, together with that of his son, who there was initiated in that scheme of planting and settling, which in later years, made the western wilderness blossom as the rose, and gave to myriads a country and a home in Pennsylvania.

The disaster which had followed the pell-mell fighting of the land soldiers at sea, now as in the time of Cromwell, prompted those in chief author-ity to place the fleet under *admirals*, men who were trained sailors, and whose nautical skill em-powered them to cope with the Dutch as well in manœuvring, as in the mere fighting of a fleet.

Both the king and the Duke of York fixed upon Penn, to command at sea in 1668.

The admiral was much perplexed at this deci-sion, for not only was his health broken by severe attacks of gout, but he also knew that the military faction would oppose his appointment, and that if carried it would be in the very face of Prince Rupert, who himself expected to receive the com-mand of the fleet. These considerations induced

Penn, since there was a state of peace, to request a further indulgence from sea service; this, however, the king declined, and it soon became known that Penn was to have a chief command. But what the king and court would not grant, the military faction enforced. Monk had sworn "that Penn should never go out with the fleet again;" but how to balk king, duke, and court? all for Penn: it was done by using Parliament as a block.

By obtaining Sir William's impeachment they prevented his going to sea, which end being gained the prosecution of the arraignment was dropped.[1]

The king, who had ever held in high esteem the abilities of Sir William Penn, and remembered his great services with gratitude, was about to raise

[1] The charges were, conspiracy to defraud, and embezzlement of prize funds. Penn stoutly denied these accusations, and as the prosecution itself had to acknowledge that whatever was done had been accomplished through orders from a source higher than Penn, and then abandoned the case, we may infer that the impeachment was but a trick of his enemies to keep him in England until it was too late for him to take command of the fleet, which view is strengthened by the fact that out of nine flag-officers against whom this suit might have been brought, he alone was selected, he, the very man whom the king, in opposition to the faction's wishes, had intended for the command at sea. That the above was the view generally entertained at the time, is evident from Pepys's assertions.

him to the peerage, with the title of Viscount Weymouth, when his son's open protest against such vanities checked the royal favor, and wounded to the soul the time-worn warrior.

Terrible indeed must have been the blow to the proud, ambitious, heart of the admiral, that his only son, on whom should accumulate the glories of his victories, had cast all aside, and turned to wander with those despised people the Quakers. At first he was indignant, and drove his son from his presence ; then, feeling his end approaching, he called him to his side, and resigning all his cherished hopes and ambitions, gave way to his natural love as a father, quenching regret in admiration for his son's integrity of purpose and indomitable will, which, in the end, raised to both a prouder and more enduring monument than any in the gift of kings.

"Son William," said the dying man, "I am weary of the world ; I would not live over my days again, if I could command them with a wish. Three things I commend unto you. First, let nothing in the world tempt you to wrong your conscience. Secondly, whatever you design to do, lay it justly, and time it seasonably. Lastly, be not troubled by disappointments. Bury me by my mother: live all in love; shun all manner of evil; and I pray God to bless you all, and he will bless you."

And so the soul of this brave admiral breathed itself away in benedictions. He expired on the 16th of September, 1670, in the 50th year of his age.

In accordance with his touching request, his body was taken to Bristol, and thus borne to its resting place in the church of St. Mary Redcliffe. First came a detachment of foot soldiers, then three large streamers on which were quartered his arms, then came his crest, helmet, shield and gauntlets, which were followed by the hearse drawn by six horses, while at the head of the coffin was the red flag of a sea-general, with those of admiral of the white and blue on each side. Long hung these banners in St. Mary's church, and still may be seen the monument there raised by the devotion of his wife.

That Sir William Penn was ambitious and worldly it is natural to suppose ; indeed it would have been strange had it been otherwise, considering the time and conditions of his life, but that his character bore the blemishes attributed to it by Pepys, cannot be believed. I have before remarked that while he was unenvied his merits received their proper deserts, but when jealousy had raised up enemies, his virtues remained his sole reward, envy, hatred and malice discharging their venom upon him. It was then that he was impeached, it was then that he was cast into prison.

Mr. Dixon, in the life of his son, calls Sir William " one of the suppressed characters " of English history. This suppression did not pertain to his historic character alone, but also to his actual self. His historic suppression, arose from the general distaste of the later Williamite historians for the recording of the deeds of any of the heroes of the Commonwealth or of the Stuart dynasty, while the suppression which he suffered in actual life arose from envy of his talents, and the general dislike in the military faction, then dominant, of all naval officers. But Penn did not suffer alone; the whole navy was suppressed ; its officers cherishing loyalty, a great part of them, as before stated, seceded from Cromwell. Being unsuccessful in their efforts, however, they had to come back and make humble submission to the Lord-Protector, who thereupon, to insure their allegiance, placed over the fleet the trusty soldiers of the army. This subjection of the navy to the army not only lasted through the protectorate, but was continued in the restoration; and thus Penn, with the other admirals of the navy, while they were first in actual merit, were second in glory to the land generals who were imposed upon their fleets.

The naval history of this period should be re-written, and its true heroes receive the laurels justly theirs. It must also be borne in mind that besides the failure and subsequent submission of the fleet, there was another cause which served to place it in subjection to the army; viz, the want of a Lord-High-Admiral, and the presence of noble-men among its officers.

The English nation is never democratic; when not royal it still remains aristocratic. Now while the aristocracy entered the army, it avoided, as a general rule, the navy, and thus the governing element inspired the military arm, and the navy, without that element, and the countenance and support of some great noble as patron, passed under the sway of the soldier.

It is hard to be second in renown, while actually the first in merit. yet such was the fate of the naval officers in respect to those of the army set over them; and no single instance of this is so marked as that of Penn. When we are told that the land generals of the commonwealth and the restoration beat the Dutch admirals, but upon investigation find that they were actually beaten, save when some seaman had control, and that the greatest victories were achieved with Penn virtually in chief-command, we may know how to read the riddle, and draw out the truth, as erst was drawn forth victory by that great admiral.

The End.

www.ingramcontent.com/pod-product-compliance
Lightning Source LLC
Chambersburg PA
CBHW031247260626
47169CB00007B/2485